Cousins Are Special

By Susan Goldman

Albert Whitman & Company, *Chicago*

To Michael, John, Peter, Katie,
Nathaniel, Zachery, and
my dear good friend, Sunny Levitin

Library of Congress Cataloging in Publication Data
Goldman, Susan.
    Cousins are special.

    (Self-starter books)
    SUMMARY: When Sarah visits Carol Sue, she discovers
that they have a special relationship because they are
cousins.
    [1. Cousins—Fiction. 2. Family—Fiction]
I. Title.
PZ7.G5693Co   [E]   78-11924
ISBN 0-8075-1317-2

© 1978 by Susan Goldman
Published simultaneously in Canada by
George J. McLeod, Limited, Toronto
Printed in U.S.A.

Here's Carol Sue—she's my cousin.
She lives far away from me.

This is my first visit to Carol Sue's house.
Right away, we are best friends.

We run up the stairs to the landing
and look out the window.

Then we bounce all the way down—
and down the basement stairs, too.

We get chocolate-covered peanuts that
Uncle Bob brings home from the store.
We look in the laundry room, where
Aunt Annabelle does the wash.

"What's that hole?" I ask.

"The laundry chute," says Carol Sue.

"We throw the dirty clothes down
from upstairs."

"Let's throw our things down," I say.

We run upstairs and get
our socks and pajamas
and throw them down
the chute.

Then we run downstairs and pick them up
and put them back in Carol Sue's room.

We jump from bed to bed.

"Let's play ghosts," says Carol Sue.
We put on blankets and shout, "Ooh, ooh, ooh!"

"Not so much noise, girls,"
says Aunt Annabelle.
"Why don't you do something quieter?"

"Let's paint," I say.
Carol Sue keeps her finger paints
in the kitchen cupboard.

I paint red, and Carol Sue paints blue.

And then we both paint purple.

"What a mess," says Aunt Annabelle.
"Why don't you girls play outside
for a while?"

"Can you ride a two-wheel bike?"
says Carol Sue.
"No, I can't," I tell her.
"Then I'll teach you," she says.

Carol Sue holds the bike,
and I try to ride it—

—but I fall down.

"You can ride my old tricycle,"
Carol Sue says.

One of her friends wants to play with us.
"Not today," Carol Sue says.
"My cousin Sarah's here, but I'll play
with you tomorrow."

We ride our bikes until Uncle Bob
comes home for dinner.
At the table, Carol Sue and I sit
next to each other.

We're the first ones done.
We go into the living room and
look at the photograph albums.
"You have a picture of my grandma,"
I say.

"No," says Carol Sue. "She's not
your grandma. She's *my* grandma."
"How can she be your grandma if
she's my grandma?" I ask.
Aunt Annabelle and Mommy come in.

Aunt Annabelle says, "You and Carol Sue
have the same grandmother.
Your mommy and I are sisters. We have
the same mother.
We're all in the same family."

No wonder I love Carol Sue.
She's more than my friend.
She's my cousin.